MY BEDTIME STORYBOOK

HAMLYN

CONTENTS

Cover illustration by Victor Ambrus

Cover design by Kasa and Steel

Published 1987 by Hamlyn Publishing
a division of The Hamlyn Publishing Group Limited
Bridge House, London Road,
Twickenham, Middlesex, England

All the material in this compilation was originally published in *Storyteller*.

Copyright © Marshall Cavendish Limited 1982, 1983, 1984
This edition © Marshall Cavendish Limited 1987

Produced by Marshall Cavendish Limited

ISBN 0 600 53105 8

Printed and bound in Vincenza, Italy by L.E.G.O.

THE LAST SLICE OF RAINBOW

Jason walked home from school every day along the side of a steep grassy valley, where harebells grew and sheep nibbled. As he walked, he always whistled. Jason could whistle more tunes than anyone else at school, and he could remember every tune he had ever heard. That was because he had been born in a windmill, just at the moment when the wind changed from south to west. He could see the wind, as it blew — and that is a thing not many people can do.

One day, as Jason walked home along the grassy path, he heard the west wind wailing and sighing "Oh, woe, woe! Oh, bother and blow! I've forgotten how it goes!"

"What have you forgotten, Wind?" asked Jason, turning to look at the wind. It was all brown and blue and wavery, with splashes of gold.

"My tune! My favourite tune."

"The one that goes like this?" said Jason, and he whistled.

The wind was delighted. "That's it! That's the one! Clever Jason!" And it

flipped about him, teasing but kindly, turning up his collar, ruffling his hair. *"I'll give you a present,"* it sang to the tune Jason had whistled. *"What shall it be? A golden lock and a silver key?"*

Jason could not think what use *those* things would be, so he said quickly, "Oh, please, what I would like would be a rainbow of my very own to keep." For in the grassy valley, there were often beautiful rainbows to be seen, but they never lasted long enough for Jason.

3

me back and I'll reward you with a gift."

"Yes," said Jason. "Yes, I'll put you back, and please — may I have a rainbow of my very own, to keep in my pocket?"

"Humph!" said the Genius. "I'll give you a rainbow, but rainbows are not easy to keep. I'll be surprised if you can even carry it home. Still, here you are." And the Genius leapt out of Jason's pail, in a high soaring leap, back into its waterfall, and, as it did so, a rainbow poured out of the spray and into Jason's pail.

"Oh how beautiful!" And Jason took the rainbow, holding it in his two hands like a scarf, and gazed at its dazzling colours. He rolled it up carefully, and put it in his pocket. Then he started walking home.

"A rainbow of your own? That's a hard one," said the wind. "A very hard one. You must take a pail and walk up over the moor till you come to Peacock Force. Catch a whole pailful of spray. That will take a long time. But when you have the pail full to the brim, you may find something in it that might give you a rainbow."

Luckily the next day was Saturday. Jason took a pail, and his lunch, and walked over the moor to the waterfall that was called Peacock Force — because the water, as it dashed over the cliff, made a cloud of spray in which wonderful peacock colours shone and glimmered.

All day Jason stood by the fall, getting soaked, catching the spray in his pail. At last, just at sunset, he had the whole pail filled up, right to the brim. And now, in the pail, he saw something that swam swiftly round and round — something that glimmered in brilliant rainbow colours.

It was a small fish.

"Who are you?" said Jason.

"I am the Genius of the waterfall. Put

There was a wood on his way, and in a dark place among the trees he heard somebody crying pitifully. He went to see what it was and found a badger in a trap.

"Boy, dear boy," groaned the badger. "Let me out, or men will come with dogs and kill me."

"How can I let you out? I'd be glad to, but the trap needs a key."

"Push in the end of that rainbow I see in your pocket. You'll be able to wedge open the trap."

Sure enough, when Jason pushed the end of the rainbow between the jaws of the trap, they sprang open, and the badger was able to clamber out. "Thanks, thanks," he gasped, and then he was gone down his hole.

5

Jason rolled up the rainbow and put it back in his pocket. But a large piece had been torn off by the sharp teeth of the trap, and it blew away.

On the edge of the wood was a little house where old Mrs Scagell lived. She had a very sour nature. If children's balls bounced into her garden, she baked them in her oven until they turned to coal. And everything she ate was black — burnt toast, black tea, black olives. She called to Jason, "Boy, will you give me a bit of that rainbow I see sticking out of your pocket? I'm very ill. The doctor says I need a rainbow pudding to make me better."

Jason did not much want to give Mrs Scagell a bit of his rainbow, but she did look ill. So, rather slowly, he went into her kitchen, where she cut off a large bit of the rainbow with a breadknife. Then she made a stiff batter with hot milk and flour, stirred in the piece of rainbow, and cooked it.

She let it get cold and cut it into slices and ate them with butter and sugar. Jason had a small slice too. It was delicious.

"That's the best thing I've eaten for a year," said Mrs Scagell. "I'm tired of black bread. I can feel this pudding doing me good."

She did look better. Her cheeks were pink and she almost smiled. As for Jason, after he had eaten his small slice of pudding he grew three inches. "You'd better not have any more," said Mrs Scagell.

Jason put the last piece of rainbow in his pocket.

There was not a lot left now.

As he drew near the windmill where he lived, his sister Tilly ran out to meet him. She tripped over a rock and fell, gashing her leg. Blood poured out of it, and Tilly, who was only four, began to wail. "Oh, my leg! It hurts dreadfully! Oh Jason, please bandage it, *please!*"

Well, what could he do? Jason pulled the rest of the rainbow from his pocket and wrapped it around Tilly's leg. There was just enough. He tore off a tiny scrap, which he kept in his hand.

Tilly was in rapture with the rainbow round her leg. "Oh! How beautiful! And it's stopped the bleeding!" She danced away to show everybody.

Jason was left looking rather glumly at the tiny shred of rainbow between his thumb and finger. He heard a whisper in his ear and turned to see the west wind frolicking, all yellow and brown and rose-coloured.

"Well?" said the west wind. "The Genius of the waterfall did warn you that rainbows are hard to keep! And even without a rainbow, you are a very lucky boy. You can hear my song, and you have grown three inches in one day."

"That's true," said Jason.

"Hold out your hand," said the wind. Jason held out his hand, with the piece of rainbow in it, and the wind blew as you blow on a fire to make it burn bright. As it blew, the piece of rainbow grew and grew, until it lifted up, arching into the topmost corner of the sky. Not just a single rainbow, but a double one, with a second rainbow underneath that, the biggest and most brilliant that Jason had ever beheld. Many birds were so astonished at the sight that they stopped flying and fell, or collided with each other in mid-air.

Then the rainbow melted and was gone.

"Never mind!" said the west wind. "There will be another rainbow tomorrow. And if not tomorrow, next week."

"And I did have it in my pocket," said Jason. And he went inside for his tea.

THE KIND SCARECROW

Farmer Furrow put up a scarecrow to scare the crows away from his barley. He made the body of sacking stuffed with straw, and dressed it in an old overcoat with brass buttons. Scarecrow's hair, too, was made of golden straw.

When the warm breezes blew, the coat flapped wildly, and the crows shrieked and rose up in a great black cloud. Angrily they flew off to the woods. The green barley shoots pushed towards the sun, and Scarecrow felt proud that he had protected them.

But there were other birds nearby whom he did not want to frighten.

High up in the sky, the skylark sang so wonderfully. The mottled thrush chirruped and hopped around Scarecrow's feet in search of worms. And a tiny blue-tit swung on his shoulder, calling out in a tinkling voice, as she chatted with him.

One day Blackbird said, "I'm building a nest, but there's so little straw these days. Could you spare me a little?"

"Of course. Take some of my hair," said the kind Scarecrow.

The other birds were building, too. So Scarecrow gave some straw to Skylark and to Thrush. Soon he was quite bald.

Then Magpie, who was bigger than the others, settled on Scarecrow's arm and flicked his long tail. He stared greedily at the coat butons. "How they shine!" said Magpie. "I do so love bright, pretty things.

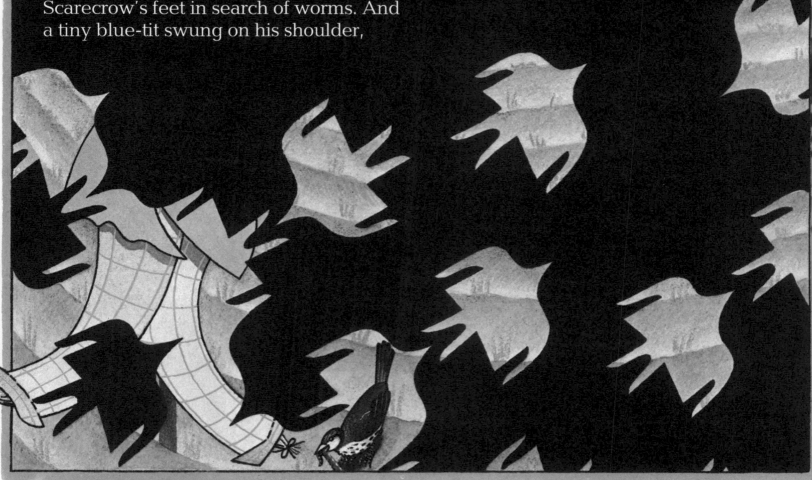

I was going to decorate my home with milk-bottle tops — but with brass buttons I'd be the envy of the whole neighbourhood!"

"I don't really need buttons," said Scarecrow kindly, and he let Magpie peck off every one of them. But then his coat would not stay fastened and he felt foolish, with his head so bald and his coat hanging open. He wondered if the birds would laugh at him, but they were far too busy building their nests.

Skylark built a nest in the grass. Blackbird found an oak tree. Thrush settled in a hawthorn hedge. Only Blue-tit was homeless. "How I wish I had a little nest," she told Scarecrow tearfully, "of moss and wool and feathers."

"My pocket would make a lovely nest," whispered Scarecrow. "And I could watch over the eggs for you." With a happy cry, Blue-tit flew off in search of moss. She flew over the head of Farmer Furrow as he came into the field.

Farmer Furrow tied Scarecrow's coat with the twine, and put the hat on his head. "All that hat needs is a feather!"

When the Farmer had gone, the birds gathered to admire Scarecrow's hat.

"I heard what Farmer Furrow said," sang Skylark. "Here's one of my best white feathers for your hat." She plucked a feather from her breast and tucked it inside the hatband.

Blackbird added a glossy black feather, and Thrush, a feather of mottled brown. They had all felt rather ashamed of taking so much straw. Blue-tit plucked out her best feathers of blue and primrose-yellow.

He stopped and stared at Scarecrow. "We can't have you looking like that, my lad, with your coat undone. And what's happened to the golden straw I gave you for hair?"

Farmer Furrow went to the farmhouse and found a length of twine and his wife's old hat. It was rather a fine hat, with a red hatband.

Thrush called sharply, "Magpie! Surely you can spare a feather in return for all those shiny brass buttons!" And soon Scarecrow had a shiny, blue-green tail-feather in his hat.

When Farmer Furrow went back to the field, he was amazed to see Scarecrow's hat so gay with feathers. On Scarecrow's shoulder perched a proud Blue-tit, and from the deep pocket of his coat came the "Cheep-cheep" of tiny, newly-hatched birds.

"Bless my soul! I wanted you to scare away the birds — not make friends with them!" said the Farmer. But he was a kind man, and the barley stood tall and thick. So he gave a chuckle and went to tell his wife.

A GREAT ESCAPE

Long ago, when the ticking of time had barely begun, the world was wild and dangerous. It was foolish to venture far from home. But one small frog had strayed from the safety of his pool. Like the drip-dripping of water drops, the little frog's heart beat in his chest as he felt the ground softly tremble. Something was coming through the scrub!

The sound was so close and the pool so far away. "Perhaps I should crouch still and pretend to be a stone," thought the little frog.

But as he looked back a huge lizard burst out of the scrub, heading straight for him! In zig-zagging leaps the frog set off for his pool, the scuttling lizard getting closer every moment.

Ahead of him the lizard saw the frog, but he was not thinking of food. Inside his scaly chest, his heart was leaping, for he had heard behind him the running feet of a human being. And looking round he saw the two-legged hunter running, with a stick in her hand. "I could crouch still and pretend to be a rock," thought the lizard, "but humans are too clever. She'd spot me and kill me and roast me over her camp fire." So he scuttled on, and behind him the shrieking human got closer and closer with every stride.

The little girl saw the lizard ahead of her. But she was not thinking of food. Inside her narrow chest, her heart was rapping like a fist. For behind her she had seen one huge horn slash down the long grass, the hooves gouge holes in the ground, and she heard a bellow of rage as the woolly rhinoceros thundered after her. She ran and ran, but with every step the rhino got closer.

Ahead of him, the woolly rhinoceros saw the little girl. But he was not thinking of trampling her — only of getting away.

Inside his leathery chest, his heart banged like a drum. He had heard the roar, and seen the flash of golden fur among the trees. A tiger was coming after him! And though his hurtling gallop shook the ground like an earthquake, he knew that the tiger was faster, gaining with every bound.

Ahead of him, the sabre-toothed tiger saw the rhinoceros. But he was not thinking of food. Inside his velvet chest his heart pounded like a hammer. For his golden nostrils had smelled the smell behind him, and his swivelling ears heard the crackling in the trees. Behind him came the biggest and fastest enemy of all — fire!

It gained and it gained and it gained on the tiger, on the woolly rhinoceros and the little girl, on the lizard and the frog. It devoured trees and bushes. It washed away the grass in a flood of flame. The whole space between sky and earth was filled with smoke. All at once, the creatures were not running away from each other. They were all running away from the fire.

The frog reached its pool and dived in. The lizard jumped in behind. The little girl threw herself into the water. And the rhinoceros — who could not stop — hurtled straight in up to his neck. Last of all, the tiger — swimming head-up, eyes shut and ears flicking — paddled to the heart of the pool.

Round the pool and over their heads,

We thought the fire must have killed you! How clever of you to hide in the water!"

They pulled the little girl out and shook their spears at the animals trapped in the pool. The beasts turned this way and that, but found every escape blocked by a warrior with a spear. "Look, Washuma! Thanks to the fire there'll be roast lizard to eat, and ten new shields of rhino hide, and a rug of golden fur for you to sleep under!"

"No!" said Washuma in a loud voice. "These animals took shelter from the fire just like I did. Listen and you'll hear their hearts beating with fear just like mine."

"Washuma! We are hunters!" cried her father, shaking his spear.

But tears ran down Washuma's face. "*Please.* Don't kill them. Let them go this time. The fire made them like brothers to me. Please don't kill my brothers!"

So the lizard and the woolly rhinoceros and the sabre-toothed tiger were allowed to go their separate ways across the plain, and Washuma went home to a great feast.

As for the frog, it sat very still on the scorched brink of the pond and pretended to be a stone.

the fire raged. Great flapping flags of flame shook in their faces and scorched the eyebrows of the little girl and the wool of the rhinoceros.

And the the fire was gone, into the distance, destroying everything in its path and driving whole herds ahead of it. All round the pool the plants were black, smoking, dead.

The creatures in the pool looked round at one another, and none of them moved. The ripples on the pool died away, and only their eyes watched and their hearts beat. The tiger growled.

Suddenly, through the smoke came a howling and hooting, and a drumbeat like a thumping heart. A dozen tall men raced up to the pool and shook their spears in delight. "Washuma! You're alive!

HEDGE'S PROBLEM TREE

Tree was always moaning, and Hedge was getting very tired of it. As trees go, Tree was small — only a crab apple tree, and not much bigger than Hedge. He was not very grand, for his branches were black and twisted, his fruits bitter little apples that nobody wanted.

It was Spring, and Tree was still moaning. "It's going to rain later today and probably most of tomorrow. The wind's going to blow, too. He might even break some of my branches . . ."

"But the wind brings warmer weather," said Hedge.

"What's more," Tree went on, ignoring Hedge, "those horrible birds will be nesting soon, eating our buds . . ."

"I'm getting tired of your moaning, Tree. If you have nothing good to say, I'd prefer you said nothing at all."

Tree muttered moodily to himself, looking around for more gloomy things to moan about. The field would soon become muddy, and the cows were sure to break the hedge, and the crows would flock into the field. The gate would be left open and sheep would be sure to come in. In May, far too many rabbits would come

and cause all kinds of havoc. Worst of all, they would make it difficult for Tree to do what he liked doing best . . . which was thinking of things to moan about.

Hedge decided something really had to be done about Tree's complaining. But what?

Now, Hedge's best friend was Old Crow, who liked hopping among her different shrubs and plants looking for worms and scaring off blackbirds and bluetits. When he got tired of that, he would perch on top of Hedge, enjoying the view and chattering.

One day, when Old Crow came by, Hedge explained her problem. "How *can* I stop Tree moaning?"

Crow had a think. Eventually he said, "Tree's got no reason for living. That's why he complains so much."

"But where do you find a reason for living?" asked Hedge.

"Usually right under your nose."

Spring gave way to Summer, and Hedge grew green and full. As usual, wild honeysuckle grew among her leaves, entwining its scented flowers. Bumble-bees hummed in the warm evening air.

"Tree," said Hedge boldly one day. "What's the most terrible thing about your whole life?"

Tree was struck dumb by the question. There were so many things . . . and he started to make a list of them.

"No, the *worst* thing."

Tree was silent for days. Finally, he whispered in a very sad voice, "The worst thing is that nobody likes me. And they don't like me because I'm ugly. My blossom only lasts a few days before it blows away. My leaves aren't pretty, and my crab apples taste terrible."

"That's *easily* solved!" said Hedge. "I could ask Honeysuckle to grow up your trunk and all over your branches. Then you would be covered with scented flowers and thick leaves for most of the year. The only trouble is . . ."

"Yes, go on," urged Tree.

"Well, Honeysuckle isn't interested. She says you *moan* too much."

Tree was silent. Eventually he said, "If I promise to moan less, could you persuade her to grow over me?"

"If you didn't moan for a whole year, she just might," replied Hedge.

So for a whole year Tree did not moan once. Even when Summer drought came. Even when it rained all October. Even when bitter winter winds blew.

And one day, the following Spring, Honeysuckle sent out a tiny shoot. As the days passed, she grew more quickly. She entwined Tree's trunk and weaved among his branches. Her green leaves set off his white blossom in May. When the June wind blew Tree's blossom away, Honeysuckle opened her pale yellow and pink scented flowers and Tree was the most beautiful of all the trees in the field.

Tree never moaned after that. Not once. Not ever.

One Winter's day, Old Crow came by and said to Hedge, "I never hear Tree moaning these days. He must have found a reason for living. What is it?"

"Ask *him*," said Hedge.

So Old Crow flew up and asked Tree what reason he had found for living.

"Can't talk now, Crow. I'm protecting Honeysuckle from the wind."

"But she's all brown and shrivelled now it's Winter."

"She may look like that *now*," said Tree, "but she's relying on me to protect

her until Spring. Then she'll grow even bigger and stronger than last year. And the year after that, she will be so big that you won't be able to see me at all for Honeysuckle. And the scent, Crow! Have you any idea how lovely it will be . . .?"

Old Crow and Hedge were very happy. Now, and for ever more, Tree was so busy with his reason for living that he never moaned again.

DRUMMERBOY AND THE GYPSY

Late one evening Drummerboy was on his way to a new home. Tom and Madge Summers had just bought him for their riding stables at Applegate.

The horse-box began to sway dangerously, and Tom had to stop at the side of the road. When he opened the back of the box to calm the pony, Drummerboy suddenly leapt down and thundered away into the dark.

Madge wanted to go after him, but Tom said, "We'll never catch him now. We'll come back tomorrow." And they drove off, leaving the pony all alone in the night.

At first, Drummerboy thought only of getting away from the horse-box, and he thundered noisily along the hard road. Then he slowed to a trot. He felt lost and frightened, and he missed his warm stable.

Sheltering beside a hedge, he fell asleep.

He was still standing there when Billy Smith came by on his way to school the next morning. Billy was a gypsy boy, with black curly hair and sparkling black eyes. If there was one thing he loved, it was horses. His father did not keep them any more, but Billy was like the old type of gypsy with horses in his blood.

"Whoa there, feller!" he whispered, stroking Drummerboy. "We're going to be friends." The pony felt that he would be safe with the boy. But how cold he was! "Poor boy," said Billy. "We'd better get you home to Grandma." And he walked back home, with Drummerboy following.

The gypsy camp was in a field just off the main road, full of shabby cars and lorries. But one painted wooden caravan stood out like a bright flower. Billy went to the door and knocked. His grandmother opened it.

"What have you got there?" she asked, peering at the pony.
"I found him up by Luckton Road. He's very cold and I thought you might be able to help him."

She went back inside the caravan and returned with a bottle of evil-smelling medicine. "It's my own special recipe." She poured some down the pony's throat — it warmed Drummerboy like liquid fire — then she bedded him down on a pile of sacks, covered with old blankets. "He'll be as good as new in no time," said the old gypsy.

Billy settled down to stay with Drummerboy until he had recovered. He was still sitting there, stroking the horse, when his father appeared.

"What's that horse doing here?" he shouted. "Get that animal away from here! Horse-stealing's a crime, you know."

"But I didn't steal him. I *found* him."

"In that case you'd better take him to the police station in Luckton. They'll know what to do with it until the owner turns up."

"Perhaps if nobody claims him, the police will let me keep him!"

"You can put that idea right out of your head," snapped his father. "There's no room here for horses." And with that he stamped off.

"Billy!" called his grandmother from her caravan door. "Come in here! I've got something to show you."

From an old carved chest, she took out a parcel and slowly unwrapped he most beautiful bridle Billy had ever seen.

"It belonged to your great-grandfather — my father," she said. "He had forty horses, and this was made for his favourite. Now you look after it, do you hear? Treat it well and it'll bring you luck."

Billy could hardly find the words to thank her. He went outside and put the bridle over Drummerboy's head. "There, it fits perfect!" Then he sighed. "But by this afternoon I won't have you any more." Drummerboy knew it was time to go. He got to his feet, Billy mounted him, and he cantered out of the camp. With the gypsy boy on his back Drummerboy was content to go anywhere.

A path cut across the fields of purple heather towards Luckton and the police station.

Drummerboy began to enjoy himself, and he raced over the ground. Billy seemed as light as a feather on his back. They galloped uphill towards a low stone wall. How Drummerboy loved to jump! He shortened his stride and prepared to leap the wall. "Up and over!" cried Billy.

But on the other side of the wall lay nothing but the steep sides of a flooded quarry. Drummerboy was gripped by fear. The ground gave way under his feet as he landed, and he began to slide down towards the water. Billy leapt off. But the pony hit the water with a huge splash.

"He'll drown for certain," thought Billy. "The water's so deep!" But Drummerboy struggled to the ledge by the side of the pool.

Billy slithered and crawled down the side of the quarry until he was near enough to catch Drummerboy's bridle. "Easy, boy, easy," he whispered. "Keep still now. It'll be all right. Help will come."

But Billy was wrong. Help did not come. For hour's he sat there with the pony's head in his arms. Billy shouted and shouted until he lost his voice. But no-one heard his cries for help. The light began to fade as evening came.

Suddenly, overhead, he heard a dog bark. Then he saw a large black labrador at the top of the quarry. Billy called. "Fetch your master. Fetch him, boy. Fetch him!" The dog ran off and in a few minutes was back with its owner. "We'll have you out of there in no time lad!" shouted the man, peering down at the boy and his horse. "Don't worry!"

In half an hour, a rescue helicopter was hovering overhead. First one of the crew was lowered with a special sling, then Billy helped him fit it round Drummerboy.

Stables. A lot of children rode Drummerboy, but he only wore the gypsy bridle when Billy was on him. And that was not the last time that it brought them adventure.

The astonished pony could not understand what was happening. He tried to keep his eyes fixed on his young friend. Would they leave Billy down there and take only him? Up, up he went, until he was lowered again well away from the quarry. Billy did not wait for help from the helicopter — he quickly climbed out to make sure Drummerboy was safe.

After that there were cups of cocoa and biscuits for Billy, and a delicious bran mash for Drummerboy. They were both taken to the home of the dog's owner. The police, Billy's Dad and Tom and Madge Summers all called there to see the boy.

"I was taking him to the police station when we fell into the quarry," Billy told them. "He's called Drummerboy," said Madge. "And you can come and see him whenever you like."

So Billy spent every weekend and school holiday working at Applegate

THE FLYING JACKET

Professor Popoff lived with his wife in a fine yellow house by the seaside. He spent his days teaching, gardening and fishing — and most of the time he was very happy. Just two things made him miserable: one was buying clothes for himself, and the other was travelling by train to his meetings in London.

One fine morning — in fact, it was Midsummer's morning — the Professor was digging in his garden when he heard an awful ripping noise right behind him.

"Oh dear," he muttered. "I have a horrible feeling that's my jacket."

The Professor was right. His jacket was so old and worn that it had split completely in two. He could still wear it if he buttoned the front together, and put it on the wrong way round. But even the Professor realised that it looked rather silly with the split part flapping loose at the front and the row of buttons down his back.

"Oh, it's no good," he sighed. "I shall have to buy a new one." And he hurried off to see his tailor.

Now, on Midsummer's eve some naughty elves had crept into the tailor's shop . . . and put magic into a jacket

standing in the corner of the window. They had made it into a flying jacket! This meant that if anyone was wearing it and wished to be somewhere else, the jacket would at once fly up into the air.

Of course, Professor Popoff did not know anything about this. When he saw the jacket in the window, he decided to have it because he liked its green and brown check pattern. So he went into the shop to try it on.

The tailor was delighted that at last someone wanted the old-fashioned jacket.

"Oh, it fits beautifully," he said as he helped the Professor put it on. "Could have been made for you."

The Professor happily agreed. "There's no need to wrap it up," he said. "I'll keep it on and give my wife a pleasant surprise. She's been complaining about my old jacket for months and months."

The Professor paid his money and walked out of the shop feeling very proud. He was looking forward to showing off the jacket to his wife — but he thought that first he would catch some fish for lunch. So he marched jauntily down to the harbour and before long he was out at sea in his little boat.

"What a beautiful day this is," he said as he looked up at the bright blue sky.

And with a sigh of contentment he reeled out his fishing line and cast into the perfectly calm sea. He had high hopes that he would soon get a bite. But time passed without even a tug at the line — and then the wind began to pick up. Large black clouds appeared on the horizon and waves began to splash against the boat.

"Oh bother! Not only have I not caught a fish but now my new jacket is getting wet. I do wish I were at home in my garden."

The magic began to work at once. Up into the air went the flying jacket . . . with the Professor inside it.

"Good grief, what's happening? I'm flying! I'm flying towards the town. I'm over the pier! I'm over the university! I'm over my house!"

Then the jacket began to go down and down, slowly and gently. "Well I never! I'm in my garden! I can't believe it. It's this jacket — it must be a magic wishing jacket."

The Professor ran excitedly inside to find his wife.

"Look at this amazing jacket."

"Oh, that's very nice dear — much too nice for gardening."

"Never mind that," the Professor said impatiently. "Just watch this. I wish, um, I wish I were in the garden."

The Professor shot up towards the ceiling, across to the window, and then out into the garden.

Mrs Popoff had never been so surprised in her life. She rushed out into the garden and just stood there, staring.

"It's magic. It's a flying jacket," the Professor called.

"It's incredible," stammered Mrs Popoff.

"But just think, dear, how useful it will be. You'll be able to fly down to your meetings in London instead of making those train journeys you hate so much."

Professor Popoff looked a bit doubtful. "I don't know if it's a long-distance jacket."

"Well, we'll see. You'll have to practise a lot first."

"I'll start right away." And the Professor spent the rest of the morning flying in and out of the dining-room window into the garden, learning to control the jacket.

By the time summer was over, Professor Popoff was an expert. At last the exciting day arrived. He was to attempt the long journey to London to attend a meeting of professors. With a rucksack on his back he marched cheerfully into the garden and waved goodbye to his wife.

"Expect me back when you see me," he called. Then taking a big breath, he said, "I wish I were in London," and he flew up into the air.

"This is the way to travel to London," he chuckled, as he soared over the

While she was away the Professor played with the children. They were using poster paints and the Professor got very excited. "I'd really love to have some like that," he said.

"We'll give you some," said the children, "and put them in pots for you."

"All my favourite colours," he said. "Red and green and blue and yellow and purple and orange. Thank you very much."

Soon it was time for the professor to go. The delighted children watched as he took off from the playground and disappeared into the clouds. He spread out his arms to steady himself as the wind began to howl around his ears.

patchwork of fields and villages. But he had not been flying long when he began to feel extremely hungry.

"What I need is some sandwiches," he said, and began to fumble through the contents of his rucksack.

"Oh fiddlesticks! I forgot to pack any food. All I've got in here are my pyjamas and washing things."

At that moment the jacket gave a sudden swoop downwards as a silver monster roared just above him.

"Good heavens!" he shouted, almost startled out of his jacket. "It's a big plane coming in to land. Oh, how I wish I was safely on the ground with something tasty to eat."

The Professor had forgotten that the jacket would act on any wish. He got quite a surprise when he began to drift down through the clouds, down and down, until he landed in the grounds of a school. The teacher of Class I also got quite a surprise when the visitor walked into her room. She thought he must be the School Inspector — and went off to get him some coffee and biscuits.

The wind was very strong. It was so strong that as the Professor approached Newcastle it blew all his paints into the clouds. "Oh dear," he gasped, "I *do* wish I were in London." The magic worked quickly. In less than an hour he was in London addressing the meeting of professors.

"My jacket can fly faster than a plane," he thought. "I could fly back home tonight and arrive in time for breakfast."

And so, as night fell, the Professor rose above a city which was a mass of twinkling lights. Exhausted by his eventful day he soon fell fast asleep. He only woke up as he landed, with a bump, in his garden.

Mrs Popoff was delighted to see him back, and hear all about his adventures. And she had a good chuckle when, over breakfast, he read out a headline from a newspaper.

"Listen to this dear. *Coloured Rain Falls Over Newcastle. Scientists Baffled!*"

"Are you going to tell them that it was you spilling poster paints in the rain clouds that did it?" she asked.

"Oh, I don't think so, do you?" said the Professor. Let's keep it a secret. Let's not tell anyone about the flying jacket."

And do you know, they never did.

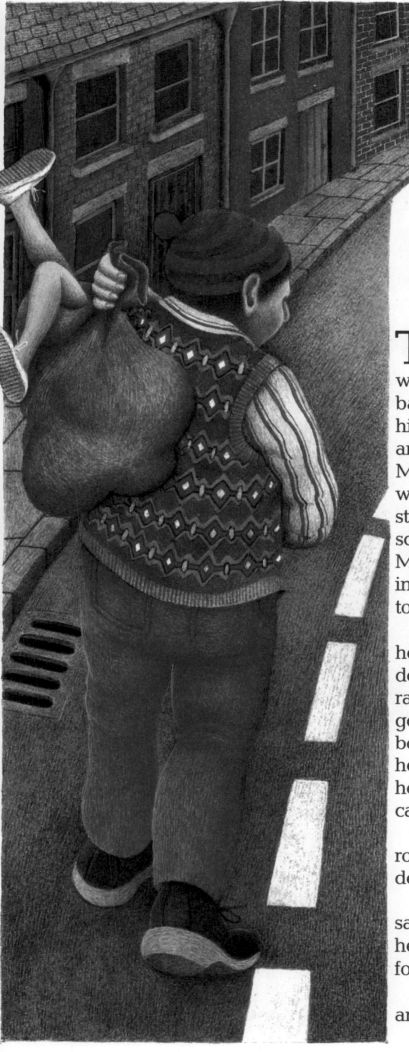

Mr. Miacca

Tommy Grimes was sometimes a good
boy, and sometimes a bad boy — and
when he was a bad boy, he was a very
bad boy. Now his mother used to say to
him, "Tommy, Tommy, be a good boy,
and don't go out of the street, or else Mr
Miacca will take you." But still, when he
was a bad boy, he would go out of the
street and one day, sure enough, he had
scarcely got round the corner, when Mr
Miacca did catch him and popped him
into a bag upside down, and took him off
to his house.

When Mr Miacca got Tommy inside,
he pulled him out of the bag and sat him
down, and felt his arms and legs. "You're
rather tough," he said, "but you're all I've
got for supper, and you'll not taste bad —
boiled. But body o'me, I've forgotten the
herbs, and tis bitter you'll taste without
herbs. Sally! Here, I say, Sally!" and he
called Mrs Miacca.

So Mrs Miacca came out of another
room and said, "What d'you want my
dear?"

"Oh, here's a little boy for supper,"
said Mr Miacca, "and I've forgotten the
herbs. Mind him, will you, while I go
for them?"

"All right, my love," said Mrs Miacca,
and off he went.

Then Tommy Grimes said to Mrs

31

Miacca, "Does he always have little boys for supper?"

"Mostly, my dear," said Mrs Miacca, "if little boys are bad enough, and get in his way."

"And don't you have anything else but boy-meat? No pudding?" asked Tommy.

"Ah, I love pudding," said Mrs Miacca. "But tis not often the likes of me get pudding."

"Why, my mother is making a pudding this very day," said Tommy Grimes, "and I'm sure she'll give you some, if I ask her. Shall I run and get some?"

"Now, that's a thoughtful boy" said Mrs Miacca, "only don't be long and be sure to be back for supper."

So off Tommy pelted, and right glad he was to get off so cheap. And for many a long day he was as good as good could be, and never went round the corner of the street. But he could not always be good and one day he went round the corner, and as luck would have it, he had scarcely got round it when Mr Miacca grabbed him up, popped him in his bag, and took him home.

When he got him there, Mr Miacca dropped him out and when he saw him, he said, "Ah, you're the youngster that served me and my missus such a shabby trick, leaving us without any supper. Well, you shan't do it again. Here, get under the sofa, and I'll sit on it and watch the pot boil for you."

So poor Tommy Grimes had to creep under the sofa, and Mr Miacca sat on it and waited for the pot to boil. And they waited and they waited, but still the pot did not boil, till at last Mr Miacca got tired of waiting, and he said, "Here, you under there, I'm not going to wait any longer. Put out your leg, and I'll stop you giving us the slip.

So Tommy put out a leg and Mr Miacca got a chopper, and chopped it off, and popped it in the pot.

Suddenly he called out, "Sally, my dear, Sally!" and nobody answered. So he went into the next room to look out for Mrs Miacca, and while he was there Tommy crept out from under the sofa and ran out of the door. For it was a leg of the sofa that he had put out.

So Tommy Grimes ran all the way home, and he never went round the corner again till he was old enough to go alone.

John and Marion were watching their father dig the garden. It was hard work and after one very big spadeful he stood up straight and mopped his brow.

"Look, Daddy has dug up an old boot," said Marion.

"What are you going to do with it?" asked John.

"I'm going to bury it right here," said Mr Martin. "There's an old wives' tale that says if you put an old shoe under a rhubarb plant it grows much better."

Marion giggled. "Will the boot grow?"

"Well, if it does, we'll have stewed boot for tea." And he buried it.

Later in the spring, gales blew down the rhubarb and Mr Martin went to pick the broken stalks.

He noticed a new plant growing in the rhubarb patch. He didn't pull it up, though, because he wanted to find out what it was

He looked all through his gardening books but he couldn't find anything like it.

"I've never seen a plant like this before," he told John and Marion.

It was rather an interesting plant, so although it had soon pushed away what was left of the rhubarb, the Martins left it to grow. It grew very well and by the following spring it was like a little tree, over a metre high. In the autumn greenish-white fruit appeared and very strange it was — all knobbly and funny shapes.

"That fruit reminds me of something," said Mrs Martin. Soon afterwards she realised what it was. "It's like boots — boots hanging up in pairs by their heel-tabs!"

"They really are like boots," said John in amazement, touching the fruit.

"Did you say *boots?*" said Mrs Tripp, the next-door neighbour, peering over the garden wall.

"Yes, our tree's growing boots!"

"Why, my young Bobby's getting old enough for boots," said Mrs Tripp. "Can I come over and have a look?"

"Of course. Come and see for yourself."

Mrs Tripp came round with her baby in her arms and held him up under the tree, upside down. John and Marion held a pair of the fruit against his feet. "Not quite," said John. "Why not come back tomorrow and see if they've grown any more."

Mrs Tripp brought Bobby round the

next day but the fruit was still too small. By the end of the next week, though, all the fruit was beginning to ripen to a shiny brown and one day a pair seemed just the right size for Bobby. So Marion picked them and Mrs Tripp put them on his feet. They were the perfect fit, and Bobby toddled up the garden path.

John and Marion told their parents about it, and Mr Martin said that anyone with babies who needed boots should come and pick a pair from the tree.

Everybody in the village soon heard about the amazing shoe tree and the next day there were crowds of women jostling through the garden gate with their children. Some lifted their babies high so their little feet could be eased into the shoes to see if they fitted. Others held their children upside down to measure their feet against the fruit. John and Marion picked those that were left over and laid them on the lawn so they could put them in matching pairs, Then the mothers who had come late sat down with the children on their laps and John and Marion went back and forth, bringing pairs to be tried on, until every child was fitted and every shoe fruit was taken. By the end of the day the tree was stripped bare.

One of the mothers, Mrs White, brought her triplets and fitted each one with a pair of shoe fruits. When she arrived home, she showed them to her husband.

"I got them free from the Martin's tree," she said. "Look, the skin's tough like leather but inside it's really soft so the shoes are good for children's feet. Isn't that clever?"

Mr White stared long and hard at his children's feet. "Take those shoes off them," he said at last. "I've got an idea."

The next year the tree produced bigger fruit, and because the children's feet had grown, they all found shoes to fit.

And that's what happened every year — the shoe fruit grew to match the growing feet of the children. Then, one year a huge sign appeared outside Mr White's house: WHITE'S HOME GROWN SHOES LIMITED it read, in large brown letters.

"He's been very secretive about that field at the back of his house," Mr Martin said to his family. "And now I see why. He's planted all those shoes we've given his children in the past few years and now he's got dozens of trees, the sly old fox."

"They say he's going to make a fortune out of it," said Mrs Martin bitterly.

It certainly seemed as if Mr White was going to make a lot of money. That autumn he hired three women to pick the shoes from the trees and sort them into different sizes. Then the shoes were wrapped in tissue paper, packed in boxes and sent to the nearest town to be sold at five pounds a pair.

Mr Martin gazed out of the window and he saw Mr White drive past in a brand new car. "I never thought of making money out of my tree."

"You never have been much of a businessman, love," said Mrs Martin kindly. "Anyway, I'm glad all the village children can have free shoes."

One day John and Marion were walking in the field beside Mr White's orchard. Mr White had built a high wall to keep people out, but on top of the wall a boy's face suddenly appeared. It was their friend, Ricky. He lifted himself over the wall and jumped

down beside John and Marion.

"Hello, Ricky," said John. "What were you doing in Mr White's garden?"

The boy grinned. "You'll see." And he ran about in the long grass, picking up shoe fruit till his arms were full. "They're windfalls from the orchard. I threw them over the wall and I'm going to take them home to my Gran. She's going to make another shoe fruit pie."

"A pie?" said Marion. "I've never though of eating it. What's it like?"

"Well, the skin's a bit too tough. But if you cook the inside with lots of sugar it's very nice. My Gran makes lovely pies with it. Come round and have some if you like."

So John and Marion helped Ricky carry his shoe fruit round to his grandmother's caravan, and they all had a piece of her pie. It had a rich sweet taste, stronger than apples and very unusual. John and Marion thought it tasted lovely and when they went home they picked some of the fruit that was left on the tree in their garden.

"Let's bake it," said Marion. "I've just learned how to make baked apples at school." Marion and John cooked their shoe fruit with raisins stuffed inside, and when their parents came home from work they served it up, topped with cream. Mr and Mrs Martin liked the fruit as much as the children did. As he finished, Mr Martin began to chuckle.

"Here, I've had a marvellous idea!"

The next day he drove his old car into town, the boot filled with boxes of shoe fruit. He stopped at the street market and spoke to a stall-holder. Then he began to unload the car. The stall-holder wrote something on a large sign and stuck it on his stall.

Soon a crowd of people had gathered round. "Look at that." "Shoe fruit, twenty-five pence a pound."

"I paid five pounds a *pair* for my little boy," said one woman. And she lifted up her child and pointed at the shoe fruit he was wearing. "Look, I paid five pounds for those at the shoe-shop. And here they are selling the same thing for twenty-five pence."

"Only twenty-five pence a pound!" shouted the stall holder. "Peel off the skins and eat the tasty flesh inside. Lovely in pies, baked or stewed."

"Well, I certainly won't go the shoe-shop and pay five pounds again," said another woman.

By the end of the day the stall-holder was very happy. Mr Martin had given him the fruit for nothing and now his wallet was bulging with money.

The next morning Mr Martin drove into town again. He saw the signs in the shoe-shops that said: *"White's Natural Shoes — they grow with your children."* But new signs had been added underneath: *"Huge reductions! Prices down to 25p a pair!"*

After that, everyone was happy: the village children still got their shoes free from the Martin's tree and people in the town didn't mind paying twenty-five pence a pair in the shoe-shops. And anyone could eat the fruit if they liked. Only Mr White wasn't happy; he still sold some of his shoes, but he made less money than before.

"Do you think I should feel guilty about Mr White?" Mr Martin said to his wife.

"I don't really think so. After all, fruit is for eating, isn't it?"

"And anyway," said Marion, "wasn't that what you thought when you first buried that old boot? Don't you remember — you promised us stewed boot for tea!"

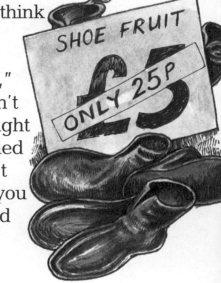

THREE BALD SPOTS

"Because I want to," I said.

"But it's hot," said Diane. "Your head will sweat."

"It's good for your hair to sweat. Sweat makes your hair grow faster, doesn't it?"

"We're going to buy a present for Marty," said Diane. "Come with us."

"Okay." But I said to myself, *"I might not go to Marty's party now that I have three bald spots and have to wear a cowboy hat."*

All my friends were at the store buying presents for Marty.

"Why is he wearing that cowboy hat?" asked the man behind the counter.

"So that his head will sweat," replied Diane.

Marty invited me and all the other kids to his birthday party. My mother said, "I'll cut your hair before the party."

"Don't cut too much!" I said.

"But it's much too long," she said as she snipped.

When I looked in the mirror, she *had* cut far too much. And she had made three bald spots on my head! *"Now I won't have any fun at Marty's party,"* I thought.

I covered the bald spots with my cowboy hat and went out to play.

"Why are you wearing your cowboy hat?" asked Joe.

asked my teacher. "I can't," I answered *"I have to cover my bald spots,"* I added, but only to myself.

I wore my cowboy hat to the dinner table, too. My father said, "Take off that hat at the dinner table." Dad's got a large bald spot. I looked at it, and decided that I couldn't explain, so I took off my hat.

After dinner I went to my bedroom, locked the door and looked in the mirror to see if my hair had grown. It hadn't. *"If I wear my cowboy hat to bed,"* I thought, *"my head can sweat all night and maybe my hair will grow."*

"Sweat makes your hair grow faster," said Joe and Diane together. *(I have good friends. They always know what to say.)*

I even wore my cowboy hat to school. "Why don't you take off your hat?"

But first thing in the morning I looked in the mirror — and I could *still* see three bald spots.

We all walked to Marty's party — first Joe with Marty's present, then Diane with Marty's present, then me with Marty's present — and my three bald spots.

We rang Marty's doorbell and his mother let us in, but she looked very cross. "Everyone's here, but Marty won't come out of his room!"

I went upstairs and peeked into Marty's bedroom. Marty was looking in the mirror and crying.

"Aren't you coming to your party?" I asked.

"No," said Marty. "I look funny."

Marty was wearing his best clothes, and I thought he looked quite good. "You don't look funny to me."

"Mother cut my hair and made bald spots," said Marty. So I looked closer, and Marty did have bald spots! Marty has a mother like mine. She had snipped too much!

I laughed, took off my cowboy hat, and showed Marty *my* bald spots. "Happy birthday, Marty," I said — and he laughed too!

So we went downstairs with our bald spots and had fun all afternoon.

Joe and Diane came round to my house. "Are you ready for the party?" asked Joe.

"Yes," I said. *"But I won't have fun,"* I said to myself.

"Are you going to wear that cowboy hat?" asked Diane.

"Yes," I answered. And, I said to myself, *"No-one goes to a birthday party with three bald spots."*

DRUMMERBOY RACES FOR HIS LIFE

Billy Smith ran along behind his father, tugging at his donkey jacket. "But we can't move away from here!" he cried. "I wouldn't be able to work at Applegate Stables at the weekends. I'd never see Drummerboy again!"

His father turned to face him. "We're gypsies, Billy. We're travelling people. Besides, that Mr Fawcett from the Council has decided to throw us off the site. It's no good, lad. You'd best forget that pony."

"But we're entered for the cross-country race on Sunday!"

"Then you'd better make the most of it, Billy. We'll be moving on at the end of the month."

When Billy went to Applegate Stables that Saturday morning, Drummerboy could sense something was wrong. He looked forward to seeing the young gypsy boy — he was always so cheerful. But today, Billy hardly spoke a word.

The Saturday morning ride was all ready to leave the stable yard, and Billy was riding Drummerboy, as usual. Just as the line of horses was about to move out, a big red car swept into the yard. The horses all snorted and whinnied with fright.

Out of the car stepped a fat, smartly dressed man with grey hair — and then a young girl. She was wearing the most expensive white jodhpurs, navy blue hacking jacket and a new riding hat.

"That one looks the best," said her father, pointing at Drummerboy. "You don't mind if my Emma takes your pony, do you boy? Good." He turned to Madge Summers, the owner of the stables, who was leading the ride. "Fawcett's the name, Councillor Fawcett. Emma will be riding here every Saturday. See to it that she gets the chestnut pony each week, will you?"

He pushed a wad of money into

Madge's hand, then drove out of the yard.

"I'm afraid you'll have to give up your ride on Drummerboy this morning, Billy," said Madge. He isn't yours, after all, and Councillor Fawcett is a very important person. He's the man who's presenting the trophy at tomorrow's cross-country race."

So Billy got off and mounted a young black colt, while Emma rode Drummerboy that morning. She did not speak once the line of horses trotted through the fields and walked along the country roads. After an hour, Madge turned for the ride home.

"You're a good rider," Billy said to Emma as his pony drew level with Drummerboy, not far from the stables.

"Daddy paid for lots of lessons," said Emma, but she did not smile or look Billy in the face. "Here he comes now, to give me a lift home."

The big car came roaring over the brow of the hill. When Councillor Fawcett caught the sight of his daughter among the riders, he sounded the car horn two, three times.

All the horses were frightened, and Drummerboy reared up, his nostrils flaring. Emma was sent over his tail, and landed on her back. The car screamed to a halt and the man ran towards his daughter.

"I'll have that horse destroyed!" he bellowed. "Stupid animal — it's obviously a killer. Look at its rolling eyes! My daughter could have been killed! I'll have that horse put down tomorrow, I promise you."

"I'm perfectly all right, Daddy," said the girl, getting to her feet. "Please! I'm *all right.*"

But it was no good. Drummerboy's fate was sealed. He was to be destoyed as a dangerous animal as soon as the vet could call at Applegate the next morning.

Billy went home to his grandmother's caravan on the gypsy site and, for the first time in years, he cried.

"What can I do, Granny? He's a good, gentle horse. Everyone knows he is. He was just frightened by that big noisy car."

"There's nothing for it, Billy," the old gypsy replied after much thought. "You'll have to do a moonlight flit."

"A what, Granny?"

"A moonlight flit, boy. You'll just have to run away together.

A gentle sobbing was mixed with the sound of Drummerboy's gentle breathing. Emma, her expensive clothes all crumpled and dirty, was holding the pony's head in her arms and crying.

"Oh Billy!" she whispered when she saw him. "Why must Daddy be so cruel? He always wants me to be the *best* at everything. He always wants me to *win*. I came here to try and save him. I thought I'd . . . I'd . . ."

"Do a moonlight flit?" said Billy. "Yeah, that's why I'm here, too. But listen, I've got a plan. You're a good rider. But are you *brave* — and can you ride over jumps?"

The two of them sat down on the straw bales in Drummerboy's box and worked out their plan. The pony, who had been frightened and restless since the disastrous ride, listened to their soft voices and felt safe again now . . . and loved.

We gypsies will be moving on soon, anyway — thanks to that Councillor Fawcett."

Billy stayed awake all night thinking about what his Granny had said. Then in the morning, before it was light, he slipped out of the gypsy site and ran all the way to Applegate, clutching Drummerboy's bridle in his hand.

It was still dark when he got there, and nothing stirred in the stable yard. But, as he opened the door of Drummerboy's stall, he could hear that someone was already in there!

Just as dawn was breaking over Applegate, they saddled him up and led him out of his stall. Drummerboy didn't make a sound. Then Emma rode him into the woods.

At midday, riders from all over the area gathered for the annual Luckton cross-country race. There were tough, wiry little ponies and tall, lanky horses. There were farmers, and riders from the local hunt. A few older boys had entered, but the course was too hard for children.

At the last minute a small chestnut pony joined the other competitors on the starting line. A pale young girl sat in the saddle, scratching the pony's head between his ears.

People in the crowd said, "She's *much* too young. Whoever is she?"

The flag dropped. The race was on. A hundred hooves thundered over fields, grassy tracks and round Applegate Hill.

The brushwood jumps were battered down as the sweating horses leaped them. Some riders fell off as the horses galloped across the river in a storm of spray.

Drummerboy had never been in a proper race before, and he was thrilled. But Emma's hands were gentle on the bridle. Billy had entrusted her to Drummerboy. Now the pony was determined to carry her safely past the finish — and get there first.

Councillor Fawcett waited anxiously at the winning post. He had no idea that Emma was in the race. He was worried sick because she had not been seen all morning.

He saw the leading horse in the race when it was still a good way from the finish — a little chestnut pony with a tiny jockey on its back in a navy blue hacking jacket and dirty jodhpurs.

"Emma!" he exclaimed. And before

he could say much more she thundered past him to the cheers of the crowd.

Councillor Fawcett hardly knew what to say as he presented the trophy to his own daughter, and pinned the blue rosette on Drummerboy's lucky gypsy bridle.

"I know how you like me to win, Daddy," said Emma in a whisper.

Madge Summers stood close by and Emma's father turned to her. "I'll buy that pony from you. He's a good little racer."

By now Madge had heard the whole story from Billy. She was very proud of the boy for giving up his chance of racing — and saving Drummerboy's life for a second time!

"Oh, I'm afraid the horse doesn't belong to me," she said, beckoning Billy over. "He belongs to Billy here. But I'm sure he'll let Emma ride the pony every Saturday."

Billy gulped in amazement. Madge had given him the pony! Madge had given him Drummerboy for his very own! But he thought quickly. He looked up at Mr Fawcett, who was trying to smile now and be friendly. "I'm terribly sorry, sir. But I'll be taking Drummerboy away at the end of the month. I'm a gypsy and the Council is closing our caravan site."

The Councillor turned pale. "Oh, um, well we, er, we can't let that happen, can we? Not when my Emma is so fond of the pony. I'll see what I can do . . ."

In the end, the gypsies did not have to leave their site — and Billy did not have to leave Applegate. He went on working there — and Emma became as good a friend to Billy as Drummerboy. Well, almost as good.

A POCKETFUL OF TROUBLE

Wilfred loved the lesson on magnetism — all about magnets and picking up pins, and magnets picking up other magnets. There's something wonderfully gluey about magnets — except that only metal things stick to them. And then the metal things turn into magnets, too!

Wilfred took a book out of the library about magnets. There was even a picture of one on the cover. But it was not as much fun. Nothing stuck to it. "I want a *real* magnet," said Wilfred. His mother only said, "Maybe for Christmas . . ." But that was far too long to wait!

So Wilfred *stole* a magnet. He picked one up in the classroom when nobody was looking and pushed it into his trouser pocket. He held his breath, But nobody said, "*Saw you, Wilfred!*" or "*Wilfred's nicked the magnet, Miss!*"

He whistled all the way to the school gates, patting his trouser pocket. Stealing was *easy*. He might even take it up for a living!

As he sat down in the park, he didn't notice the bent iron nail in the grass. It didn't hurt when he sat on it — it was under the pocket with the magnet in.

But when he got up, the nail clung to the magnet — even through the cloth of his trousers. It clung so tightly that even if Wilfred *had* noticed, he could not have pulled it away. But Wilfred *did* notice the tobacco tin.

It tore itself free of its concrete base and bowled out of the park gate. Wilfred tried to run, but the bin was too fast for him. With a clang, it stuck to the tobacco tin, which was stuck to the bent nail, which had stuck to the magnet. . .

It leapt out of the litter-bin by the park gate and clung to the bent iron nail. He was so embarrassed. People might think he smoked. He tugged and pulled, but the tin was magnetic now. It stuck fast. And then the litter-bin followed!

Wilfred turned up the collar of his blazer and hoped nobody would recognise him. But as he walked past the dairy, a milk float veered on to the pavement and — *clang* — it buffeted Wilfred from behind. And stuck fast to the litter-bin.

The milkman, who had fallen out of his float, picked himself up and shouted and shook his fist. Wilfred took fright and started to run. But it was not easy, with the nail and the tin and the bin and the milk-float hanging on behind.

It was even more awkward when the Number 14 bus joined on.

It was just about then that the Russian spacecraft fell to earth. It seemed to have been pulled out of its orbit by a *huge* magnetic force . . .

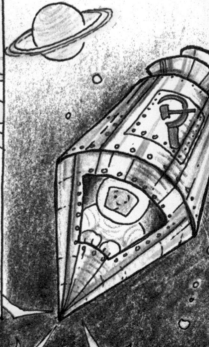

Wilfred cut across the embankment to try and throw them off. But he only succeeded in attracting the 5.30 train to London. It hurtled off the rails and clung to the Number 14 bus, the milk float, the bin, the tin and the nail.

Wilfred crawled on wearily, his blazer over his head in case he was spotted by someone he knew. And the nail and the tin and the bin and the milk float and the Number 14 bus and the 5.30 train followed on behind. So did the big, bleeping spacecraft with a hammer and sickle painted on the top. Then, just as he reached his own front gate . . . the pocket tore off his trousers.

The magnet inside clung to the bent iron nail, the nail to the tobacco tin, the tin to the litter-bin, the bin to the milk-float, the float to the Number 14 bus, the bus to the 5.30 train, and the train to the spacecraft. But *nothing* clung to Wilfred!

A great heap of magnetic metal lay in the road. And later, the men from the Council had to come and take it all away. Wilfred's mother shouted at him for tearing the pocket off his trousers. And Wilfred decided he would *not* take up stealing for a living.

Boffy and the Teacher Eater

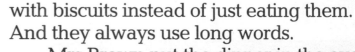

Boffy Brown was six years old. He was rather small and rather thin, with large glasses and a pale, serious face. He wanted more than anything to be an inventor.

"You can't be that until you're grown up," said his father.

"But I'm a genius," Boffy pointed out.

"Yes," said his mother, "I'm afraid he is."

Boffy's mother found living with a genius very difficult. Geniuses tend to think it's tea-time when it's only breakfast-time. And they build things with biscuits instead of just eating them. And they always use long words.

Mrs Brown put the dinner in the oven early because she wanted to start her spring-cleaning. Soon the kitchen was full of buckets and mops and dusters.

"There must be quicker ways of cleaning a room," said Boffy, and he went to his little workshop behind the cabbage patch. In no time at all, he had made a large, funny-looking machine. It had a horn at one end and a plastic sack at the other, and it was held together by rubber tubes.

"What is it?" asked Mrs Brown, as Boffy appeared in the doorway with the new invention.

"It's a Dust Extractor, of course." And before Mrs Brown could stop him, he had switched it on.

"It works!" cheered Boffy, and the awful noise drowned Mrs Brown's screams.

Brooms and mops rattled up into the Dust Extractor. A jar of marmalade flew off the table, followed by cups, saucers and then the tablecloth. Boffy was delighted, because not all his inventions worked. It moved nearer to the cooker. Lids flew off the pans and out popped the potatoes and the runner beans. They slithered down the tubes of the Dust Extractor and took the boiling water with them. Last of all, the oven doors swung open and out shot the roast pork.

"You're a disgrace!" thundered Boffy's mother.

"You'll go straight to your room and you will *stay* there," said his father that evening.

"I'm sorry," said Boffy. It was hard being so clever.

For a whole week Boffy behaved himself. He gave his Dust Extractor to the dustmen. He sat in the garden and counted the bees.

Mr and Mrs Brown began to worry.

"Do you think we should have been *so* cross with Boffy?" they said to each other. "If only he would invent something small . . ."

The next day, Boffy went to school. He was in Class 4 — because of being so clever. He should have been in Class 1, but the teacher did not want him. *He* kept correcting *her*. But Mr Grim of Class 4 had been to university, so he knew one or two things Boffy did not.

Today Mr Grim was in a bad mood. He threw a piece of chalk at Herbert Entwhistle, and made all the children stay in at playtime. He even made Jenny Green cry.

"He's horrible, *horrible*," she sobbed.

"Don't cry, Jenny," said Boffy. "I have an idea. Tomorrow you'll have nothing to worry about."

After tea, he went to his shed behind the cabbage patch and he banged and he hammered. Then he locked the shed, kissed his parents goodnight and went to bed. His small head was quite worn out.

Next morning Boffy took his new invention with him to school.

"Ooh, what's that?" asked the children, gathering round.

"It's a Teacher Eater," explained Boffy.

The Teacher Eater was very large. It was a sort of cross between a robot and a dragon. It was made mostly of tin and, on its enormous face, Boffy had painted a big smile, because he did not want to frighten Jenny.

"Ooh, he's *super*, Boffy," she said.

Boffy kept the Teacher Eater hidden under a pile of coats until after playtime. Then he wheeled it out into Class 1. The Teacher Eater trundled across the floor and swallowed the Infant teacher.

"Hurray!" cheered the children. And the noise brought the other teachers racing out of their rooms. They clapped their hands and shouted angrily. Then the Teacher Eater took a liking to the Art teacher. Her red stockings were the last the children saw of her.

"Mon dieu!" gasped the French teacher. But he had no time to say more before he was swallowed too.

The terrible machine rolled down the corridor, hungry for more. It charged here and there, gulping down teachers until there was not a single one left.

Boffy put his invention in a big cupboard and locked the door.

"Well, children," he said. "Back to your classrooms." Everyone did as they were told. They were happy to have Boffy as their new Headmaster.

Boffy went to the Headmaster's study and sat down to think.

The next day, all the children went to school early. With Boffy as their Headmaster, they expected to spend the morning playing games and the afternoon painting or messing around. But Boffy had been thinking. He pinned up a large notice in the hall. It read:

First lesson: Sums
Second lesson: Handwriting
Third lesson: Science
Fourth lesson: Serious talk by Boffy
　　　(signed) Boffy *(Headmaster)*

"What about playtime?" said Simon Goodbody, halfway through the morning.

"Work is more important," said Boffy, sternly.

"But *you're* not working," said Simon. "*You* just sit in the Headmaster's office."

"Of course. That's what Headmasters do. You can stay in after school."

Then a *dreadful* thing happened.

The Dinner Lady did not arrive. She had heard about the Teacher Eater and was too afraid to come. So the children had no dinner. And Jenny began to cry.

"I'm hungry, Boffy," she wailed.

"So are we," said Johnny and Kate, and they began to cry, too.

"And your lessons are too hard. I can't do them!"

"Neither can I!" Soon the whole school was wailing and moaning.

"I wish our teacher was back," sniffed Jenny. "I wish she was."

Boffy was cross. "You just can't please some people."

At that moment the door opened and in stamped Boffy's father. "Now then, Son. Where's the Teacher Eater?"

Boffy unlocked the cupboard. The Teacher Eater gleamed in the electric light.

"Right," said Mr Brown, pulling out the machine. "Now *I've* brought along an invention. It's not a new one, but it does work."

It was a tin opener. And gradually Mr Brown cut a large hole in the Teacher Eater's back.

Out rolled the Infant teacher, then the Art teacher, the Needlework teacher, the French teacher . . . and finally the Headmaster himself. They sat in a heap on the floor, looking dazed and crumpled. They could not think where they had been, or why. Then the Headmaster caught sight of the Teacher Eater and remembered. He turned very pale. "There will be a half-day holiday today. Good afternoon, children." And the children cheered.

Mr Brown drove his son home. "You're a DISGRACE!" he said, "and you'll go straight to bed without tea *or* supper. And you will *never* invent anything ever again . . ."

"Not until I'm grown up, anyway," said Boffy.

Then Mr Brown laughed very loudly, and Mrs Brown laughed too. And they thought how lucky they were after all to have a genius in the family.

And all the other mothers and fathers in the town thought how lucky *they* were that they did not.

NEVILLE TOOGOOD

Neville Toogood was too good to be true. He never made a noise. He helped old ladies across the road. He drank prune juice because it was good for him, and he washed at least twice a day without anyone telling him to. His bedroom was always tidy, and in school his teachers thought he was wonderful.

"Neville's a little angel, isn't he?" his mother would say. And other boys' mothers would say, 'A little angel, yes." But secretly they thought, "What a pain in the neck!"

Then one day Neville got a pain. It wasn't a pain in the neck. It was a bit further down his back — and anyway it was more of an itch. He tried to scratch it but he couldn't reach.

At bedtime he said goodnight to his mother and father, and put himself to bed. He was putting on his pyjamas when he noticed the reflection of his shoulders in the mirror. There were two large lumps!

That night, he could only get to sleep by lying on his face, and in the morning his pyjama jacket didn't fit him. He looked in the mirror again, and there they were, two small wings!

favourite pupil. Neville coughed nervously "No," he said. His teacher could hardly believe her ears. "Neville," she said firmly. "Take off your coat!"

"Shan't. Won't! You can't make me, you silly old boot!" he shouted, pulling a face. At once, a feather moulted out of his wings.

"NEVILLE!"

There was worse to come. As he cleaned his teeth (brushing up and down, of course, not across) a dazzle of light flared up off his head and took the shape of a halo. Neville was turning into an angel.

Poor Neville. The wings made his jumper lumpy, and the halo gave him a headache. "I don't want to be an angel," he thought. "I'll look such a cissy floating around in a white frock. Nobody likes me much now. Nobody will even speak to me when I'm a fully fledged angel." He put on his parka to hide the wings, and pulled up the hood to hide the halo.

But when he handed in all his homework (on time, as usual), he actually felt the wings sprout, and long white feathers dropped down below the parka. There was only one escape from becoming an angel. He would have to do something really BAD — the badder the better.

"Neville, do take your coat off, dear," said the teacher, smiling warmly at her

Hugging his coat round him, he fled out of the classroom, out of the school, and up the street. He stopped by the fire station and drew a picture of the teacher in chalk on the wall. Underneath he wrote: *'Bad is Beautiful'* and *'Wickedness is Wonderful'*. When he set off for the shops, he left behind a pile of angel feathers on the pavement — enough to stuff a pillow.

But oh, how he hated it. Being naughty was extremely hard work for a little angel like Neville.

In the supermarket,
he took away the bottom
tin in the baked beans
display. He pulled the plugs out
of the refrigerators and defrosted all
the chickens. He drove a trolley through
the paper towels, and twin-pack toilet
rolls rained down on the shoppers.
"What? Well, the little devil!" they
shouted, and manager shook his fist.

Neville felt for his halo. It had faded,
except for a warm patch at the back of his
head. And it went altogether after he had
thrown a few pebbles at the ducks on the
pond. By the time he had let down a
couple of car tyres, rung a few doorbells
and stolen some sweets from a baby, he
was very nearly having fun. A devilish
sort of laugh kept gurgling up in his
throat, and his angel feathers were falling
like rain.

"You little devil!" shouted a man
whose windows he broke. But Neville

sped on, past the Salvation Army band on
the corner *and* stole their collecting tin as
he went.

Back at home, he played trampolines
with his boots on — until the bed broke.
He got out all his toys . . . and didn't put
one away again.

"Make me some dinner, mother," he
demanded. "And do it *now*."

"Have you washed your hands,
dear?" said his mother.

"No, and I'm not going to wash ever
again, or brush my teeth — not even back
and forth."

"Neville!" shouted his father. "What's
the matter with the boy, mother? Is he ill?"

To tell the truth, Neville didn't feel at
all well. He had an awful pain in his

forehead. "Well it can't be my halo," he thought. "I haven't done anything *good* all day!"

He ran to the bathroom mirror to look. And there were two small red lumps above his eyebrows. His eyes had gone a funny colour, and he had another pain in the seat of his pants.

It was not until the next morning that Neville understood. By that time, he had a fine set of horns, and a pointed tail hung down to his knees.

Neville was a devil!

Poor Neville. He had to start being good all over again. He said sorry to his mother, returned the collecting tin to the Salvation Army, and went to scrub the fire station wall. He apologised to his teacher.

"I wasn't myself yesterday," he said. And she asked him why he was wearing a bandage round his head. "I banged my forehead," he lied — and the tailed tucked up inside his trousers grew a little longer.

Only after three days of being good did the tail and horns wash off in the bath.

Neville breathed a sigh of relief and promised himself that he would never be really naughty again. But, just in case the wings or the halo came back again, he always made a point of brushing his teeth back and forth, instead of up and down as everyone told him he should.

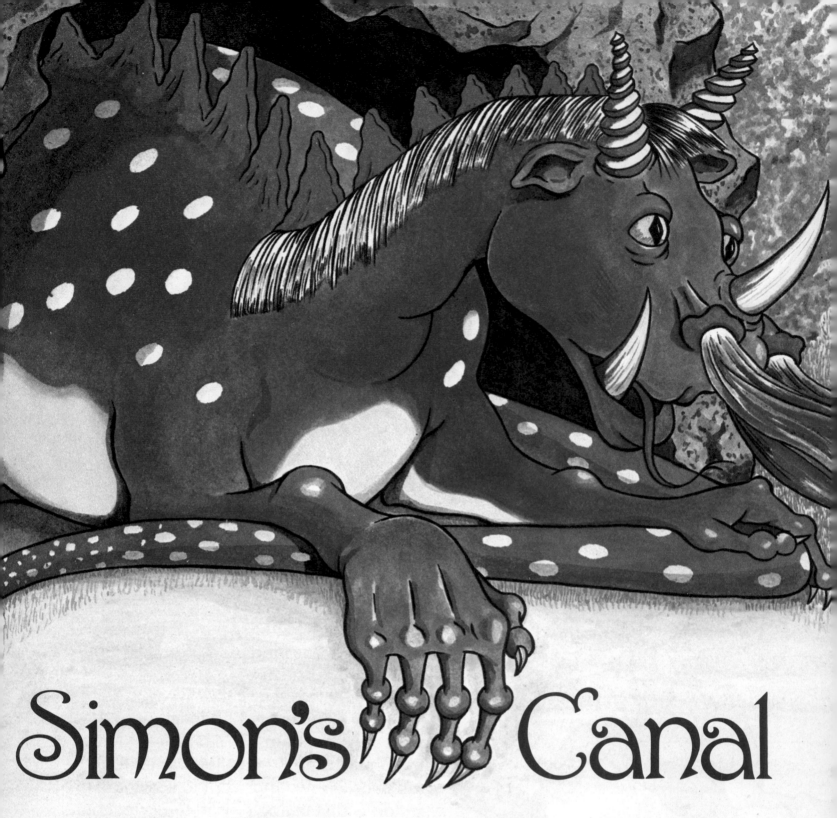

Simon's Canal

"Don't go near the canal!" said Simon's mum.

She said this ten times a day to Simon's big sisters, Trish and Paula. Trish and Paula had to look after Simon, keep him safe from harm.

Mum put on Simon's jacket and combed his hair. Then she said to the girls again: "Remember now, keep away from that canal!"

Simon did not know what a canal was. How could he know if he never saw it? He guessed it was a huge and frightening monster in a lair near Curran's Mill. Sometimes he heard it roaring. One dark, windy night it came galloping up the lane towards their house, hungry and angry. A good thing the door was locked and the curtains drawn.

Trish and Paula took Simon to the library.

"Simon can have a book with one of my tickets," said Trish.

"He can't read."

"Well he can look at the pictures."

"What sort of a book do you want, Simon?"

"A book about a canal."

"No," said Trish. "There's only one book about a canal. It's too boring. You won't like it."

Simon knew what boring meant. He had watched his dad boring holes. Perhaps the canal bored holes in people with its horns. Trish was right — he would not like that.

"Here's a good book for Simon," said Paula.

The cover of the book had a picture of a great, green dragon roaring across a river.

"Is that a canal?" asked Simon.

"Well, it's nearly the same," said Paula, thinking he meant the river.

"You and your canal!" sighed Trish.

Next day, Gran came from London for a holiday. Gran loved the country.

"We shall go out every day," she said to Simon.

When Trish and Paula were at school, Gran and Simon had fun. They went to the park. They rambled through the woods. They climbed up the hill behind Simon's house. Then, one lunchtime, Gran said they would walk by the canal that afternoon.

Simon looked startled. His tummy felt queer and he could not eat his pudding.

"Aren't you scared, Gran?"

"Scared of a weedy canal? I should think not!" said Gran.

So the monster was not frightening after all. It was growing old, losing its strength. Simon began to feel sorry for it.

Gran and Simon walked through the fields. They came to Curran's Mill.

The mill stood on the banks of the water and the power from the water ran the mill. Simon did not feel scared with Gran beside him.

"Where's the canal?" asked Simon

"Right in front of you, of course!" Gran pointed with her umbrella.

"Oh, said Simon. He could see nothing but water.

Then he knew! The monster was *invisible*. It could see them, but they could not see it. The monster hummed quietly to itself. But it did not try to hurt them. It was old.

At teatime, Simon said: "They'll never be able to catch it, anyway."

"Catch what, dear?"

"The canal."

Trish and Paula giggled. "Isn't he funny, Mum? Who would ever want to catch a canal?"

"Good!" thought Simon. "Nobody wants to catch the canal. And the canal does not want to catch us."

"I'd like another piece of cake," said Simon. "Please!"